That is 1 great idea!

MO WILLEMS'
ELEPHANT & PIGGIE
LIKE READING!

THE COOKIE
FIASCO

BY DAN SANTAT
CALDECOTT AWARD WINNER

An **ELEPHANT & PIGGIE LIKE READING!** Book

Hyperion Books for Children / *New York*

AN IMPRINT OF DISNEY BOOK GROUP

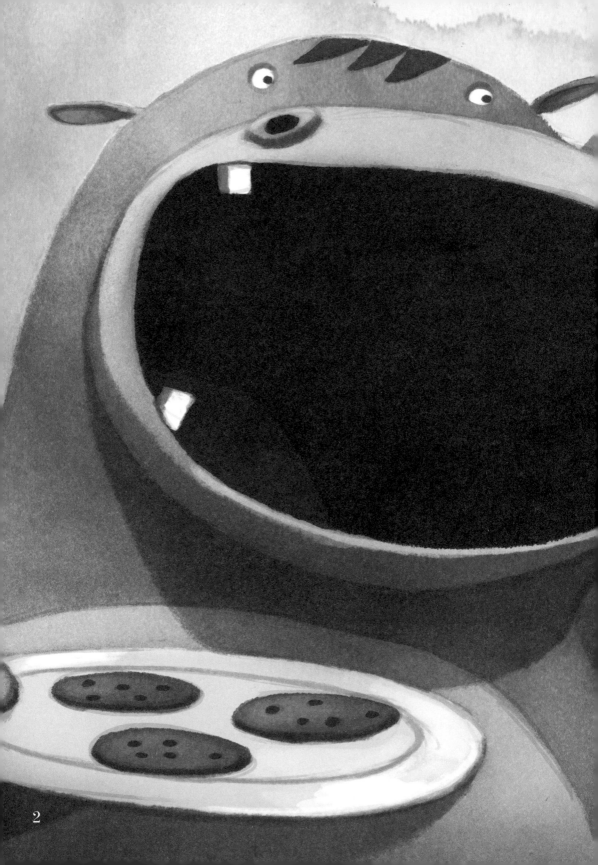

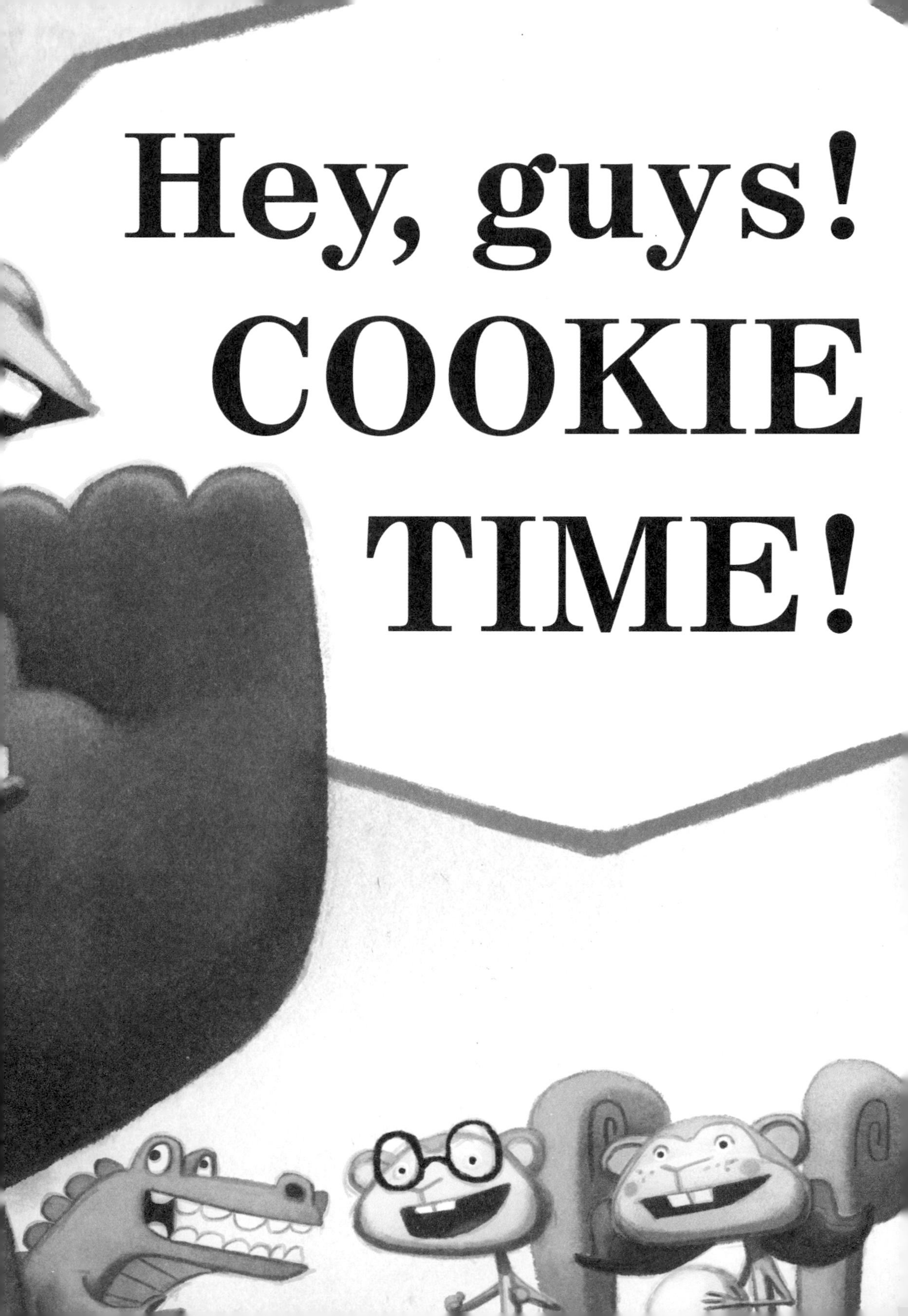
Hey, guys! COOKIE TIME!

SOMEONE
WILL NOT GET
A COOKIE!

6

7

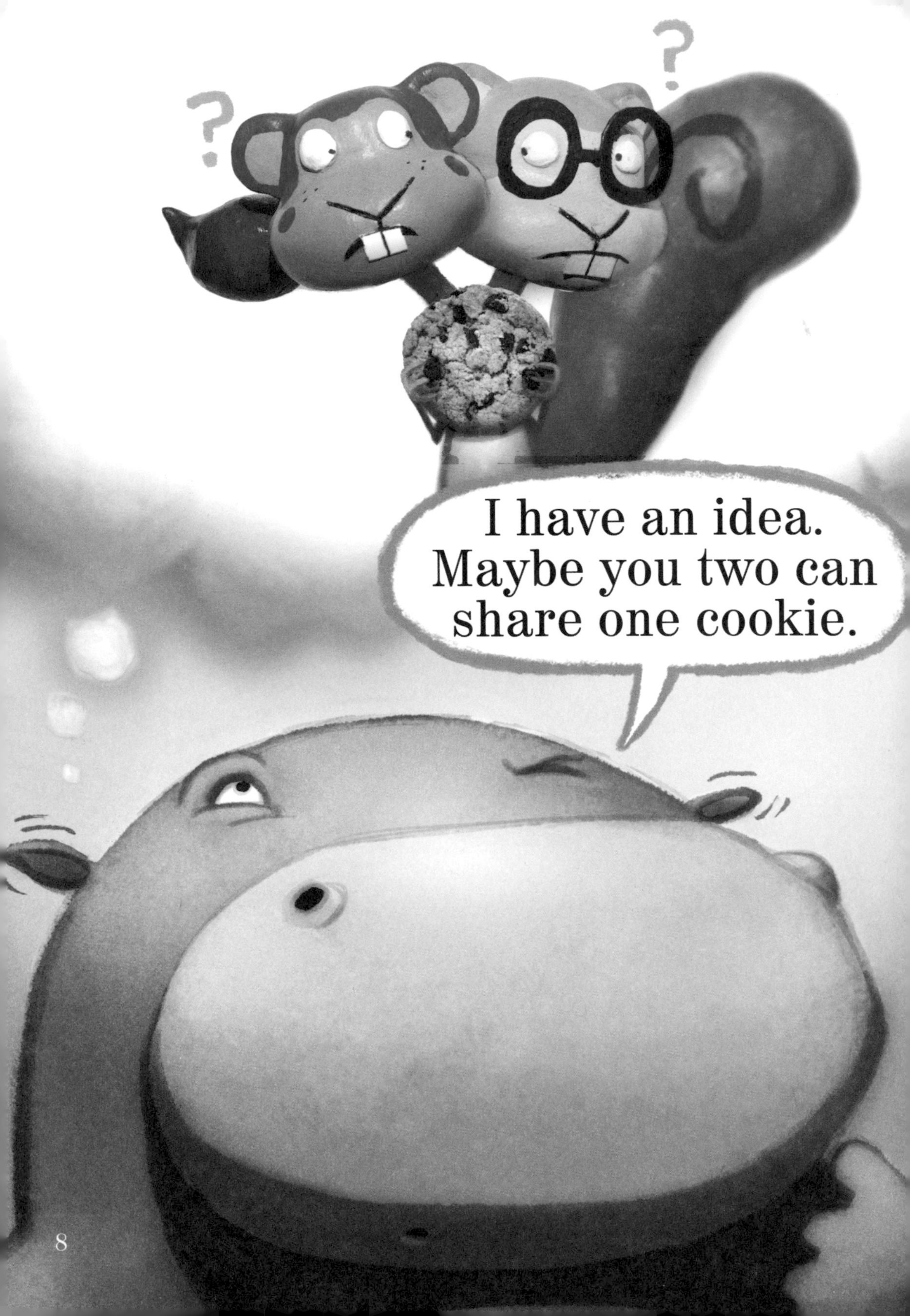
?
?
I have an idea. Maybe you two can share one cookie.

WHAT?! WE DO NOT SHARE COOKIES! WE DO NOT SHARE A LOT OF THINGS!
I *AM* wearing her socks.

I heard crocodiles do not like cookies.
Maybe *YOU* should not get a cookie!

Huh?! I eat cookies! I love cookies!

I could eat a whole plate RIGHT NOW!

SNAP

11

Or, we can share by our size.

That's a great idea.... WAIT! You are HUGE! You would get all the cookies!

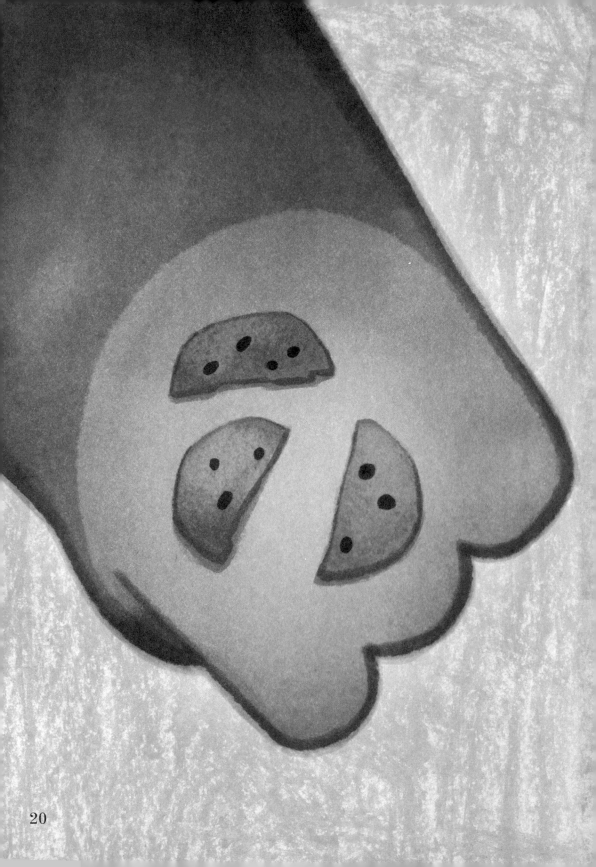

23

We have to solve this problem FAST!
Our friendship depends on it!

27

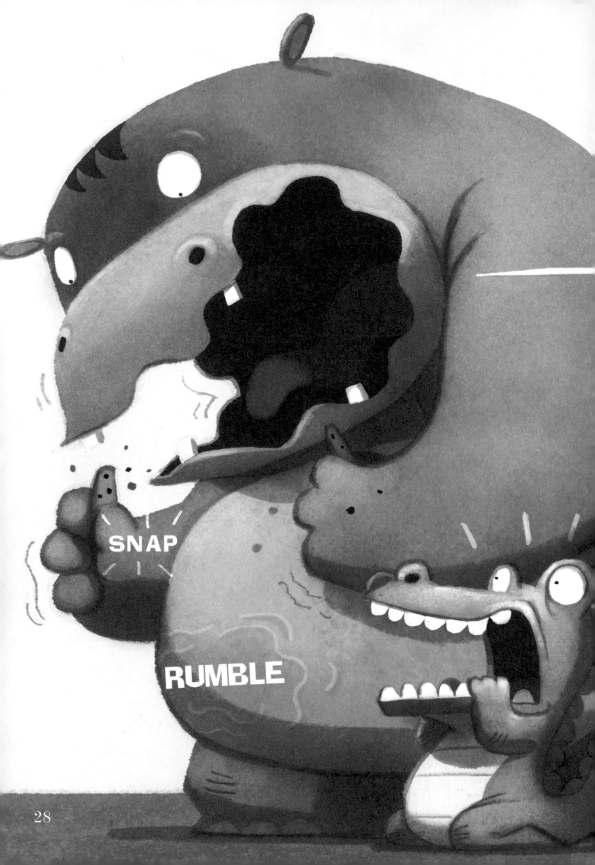

29

STOP!
The pieces are getting smaller!
They will be crumbs soon!

We will have to eat cookie crumbs!

This is a flop. A mess. A DISASTER!

It is a *fiasco*.

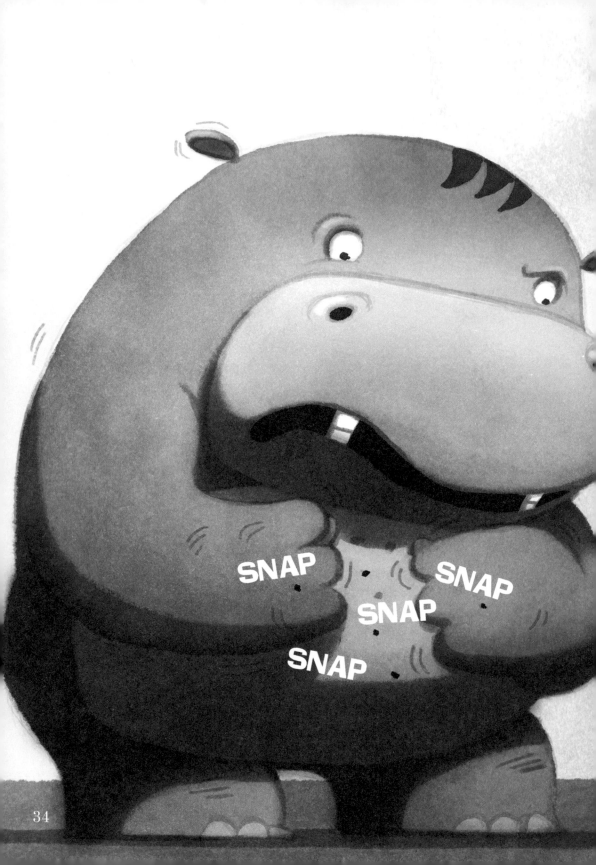

GAH! SORRY!
I CANNOT
STOP!

He broke all the
pieces again.

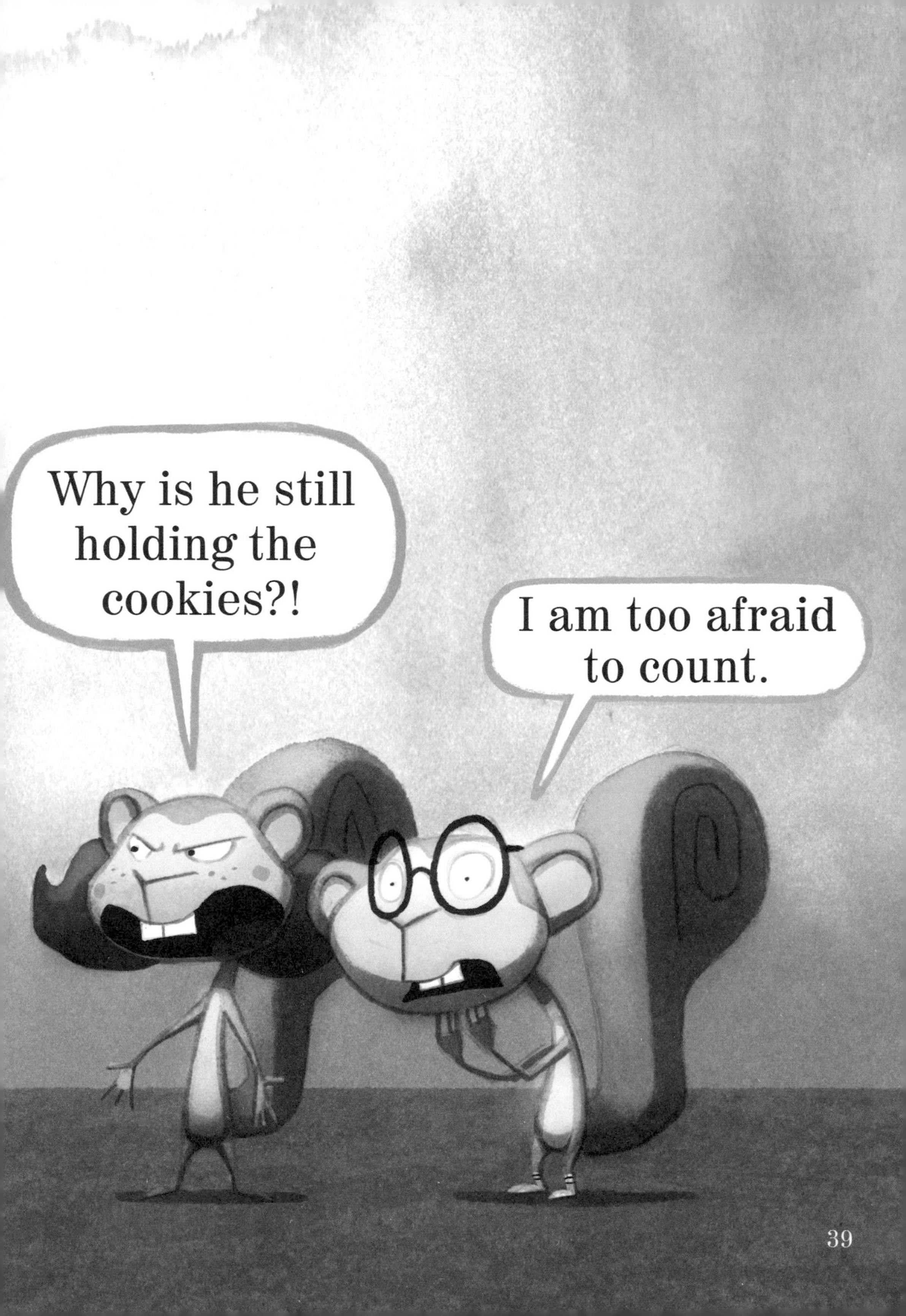
Why is he still holding the cookies?!
I am too afraid to count.

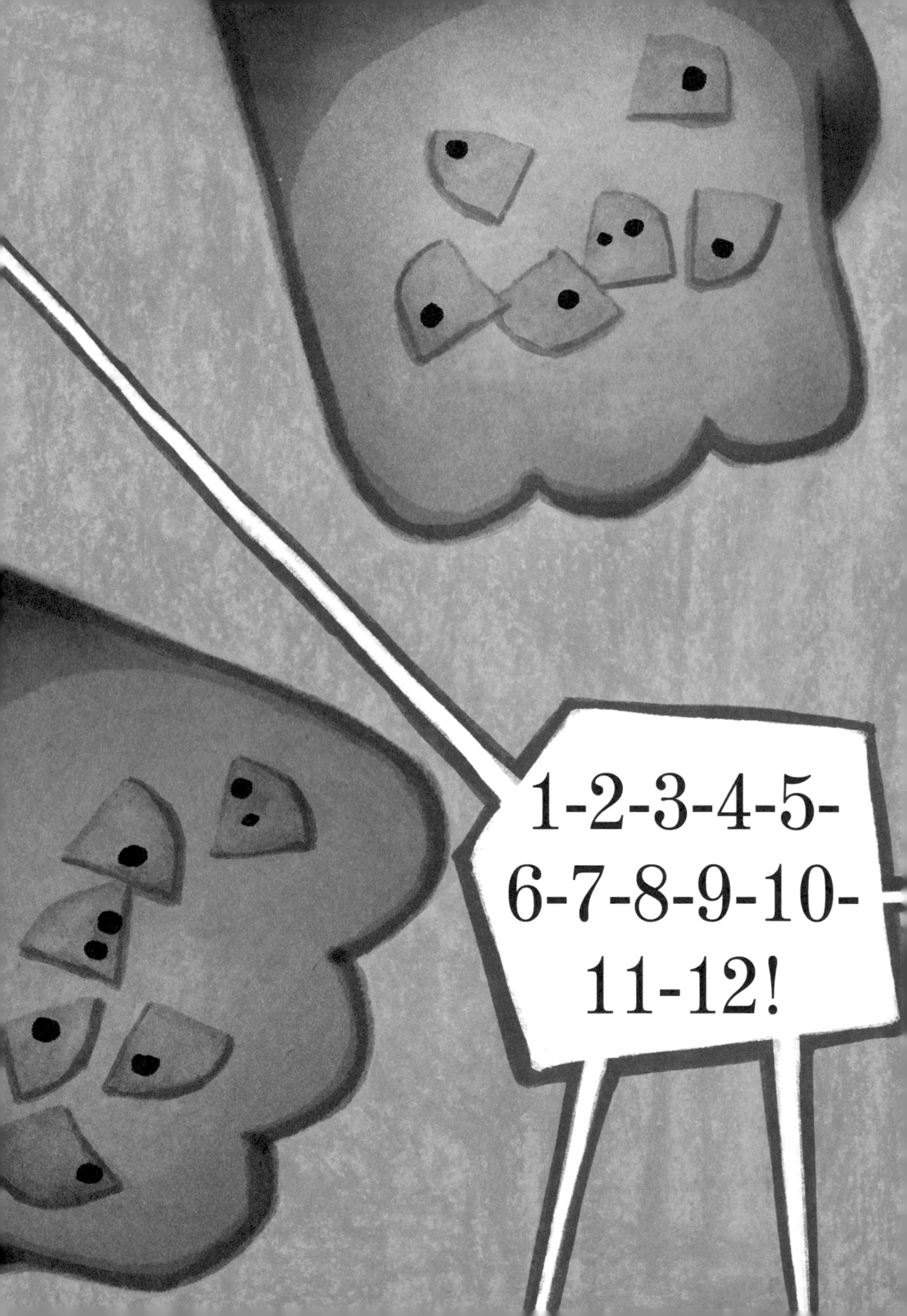
1-2-3-4-5-
6-7-8-9-10-
11-12!

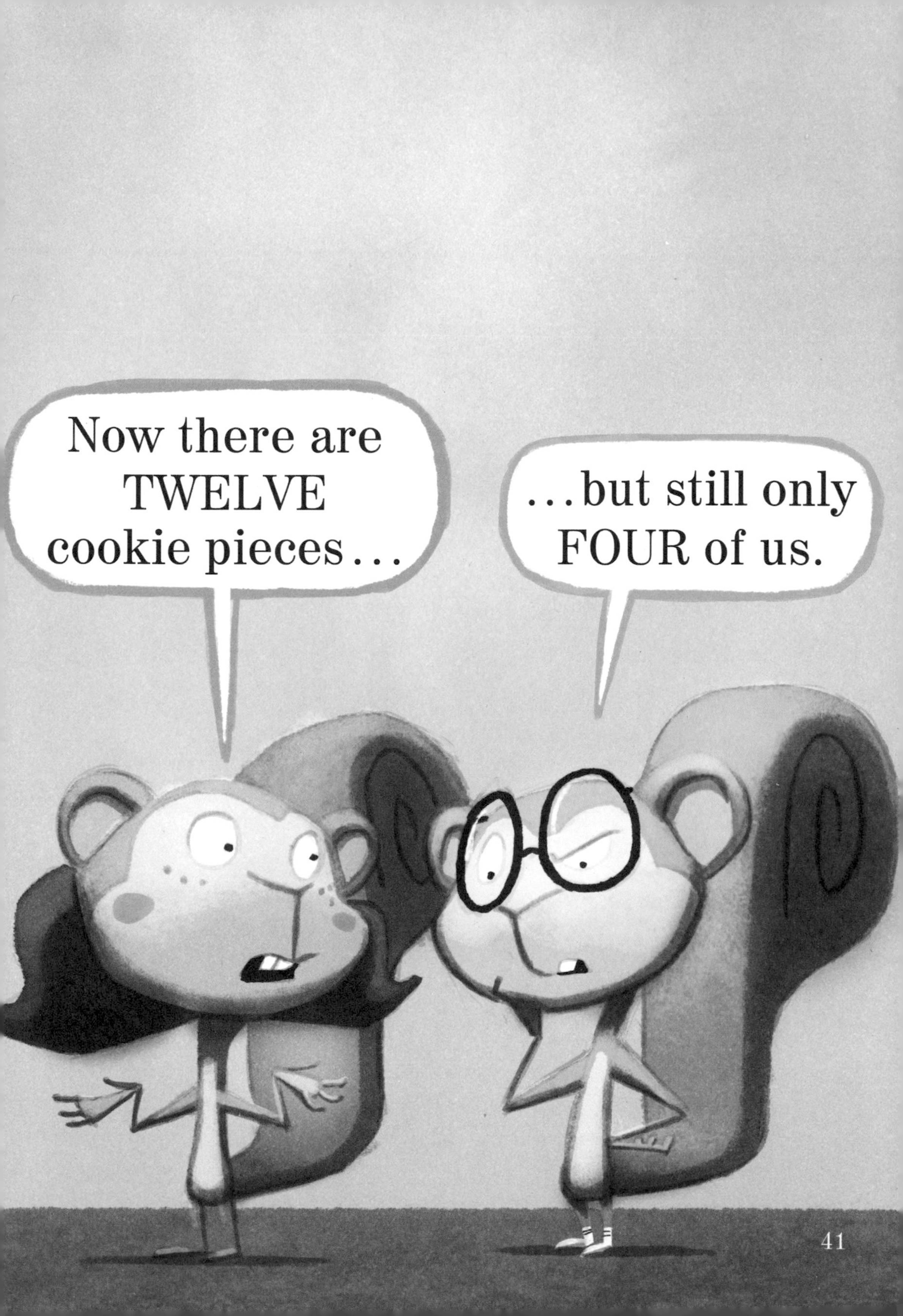
Now there are TWELVE cookie pieces...
...but still only FOUR of us.

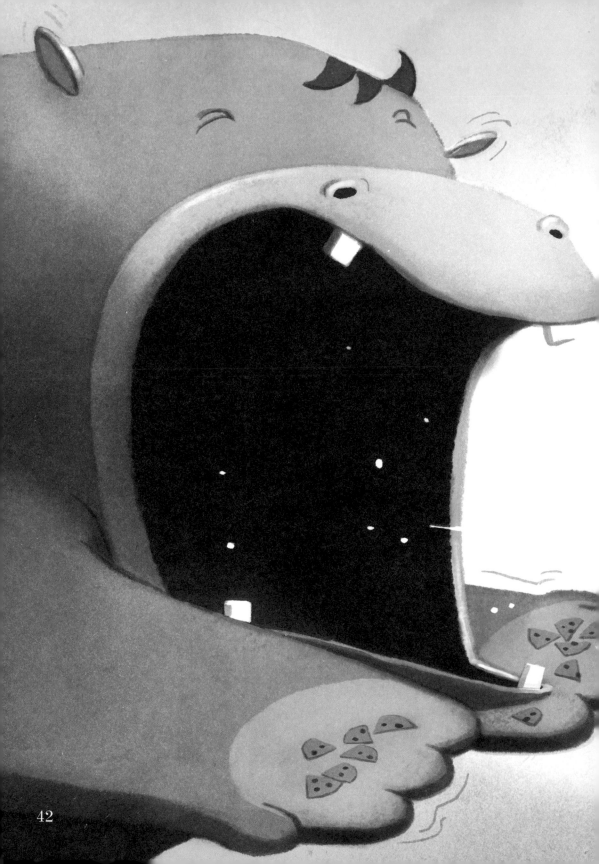

43

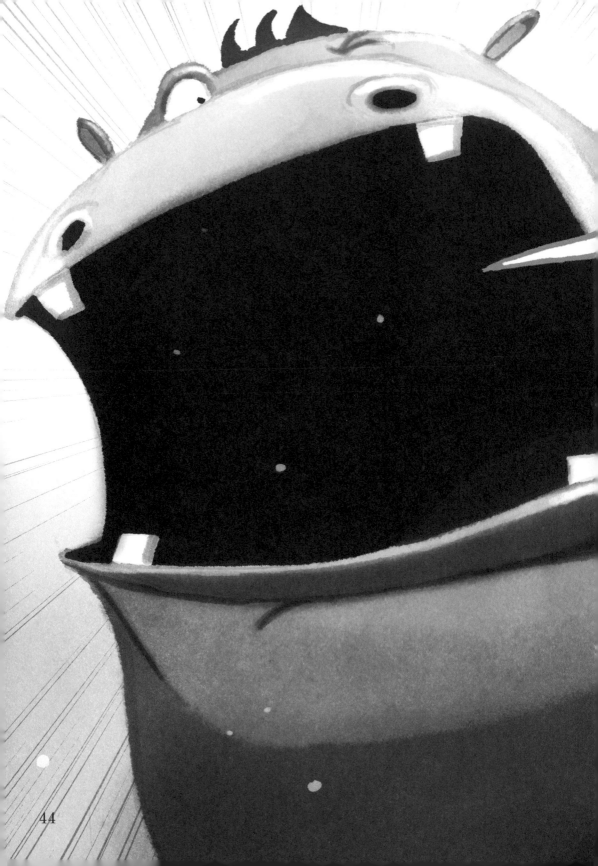

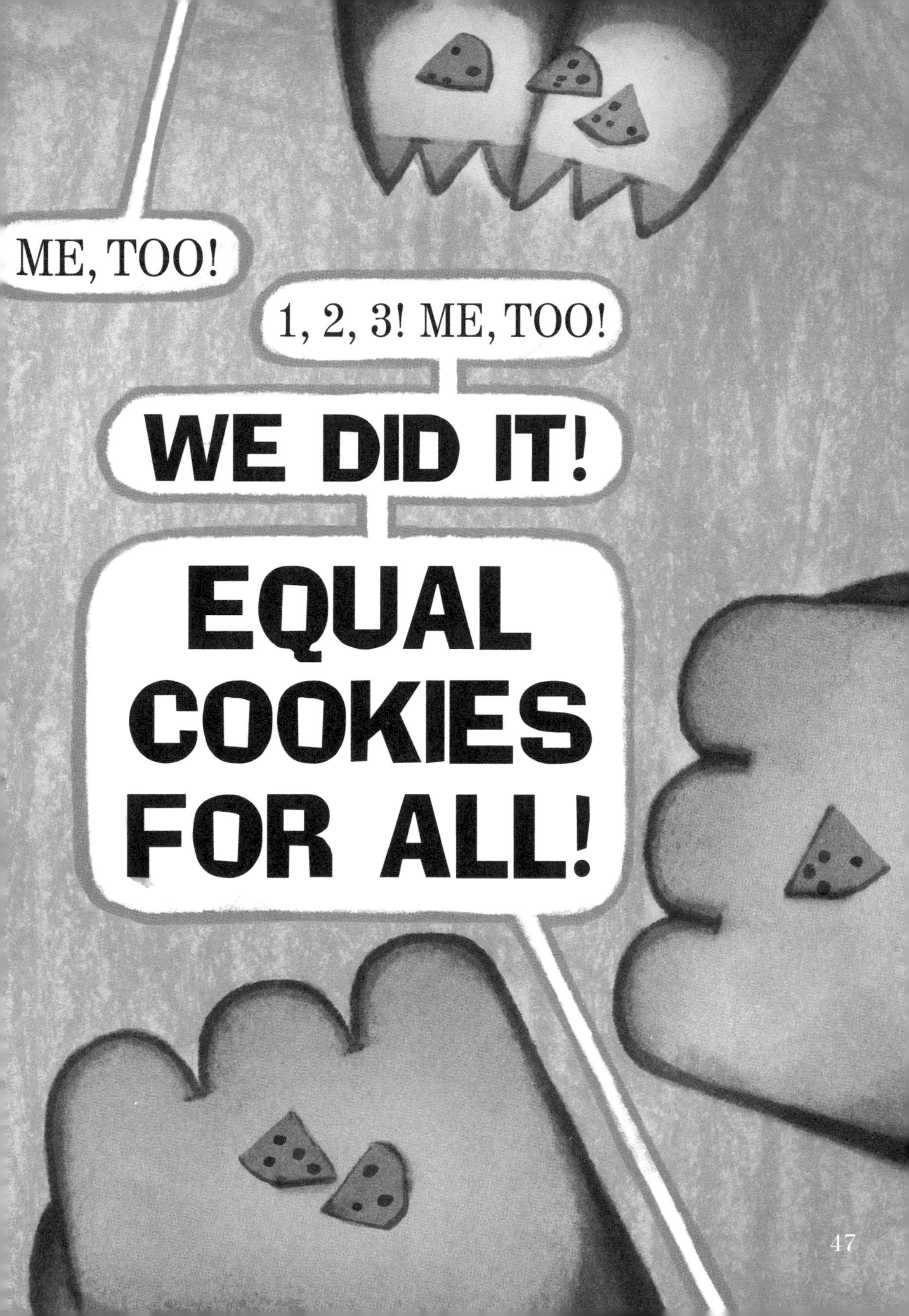

ME, TOO!
1, 2, 3! ME, TOO!
WE DID IT!
EQUAL COOKIES FOR ALL!

MUNCH
MUNCH
MUNCH
MUNCH
MUNCH
MUNCH
MUNCH
MUNCH
MUNCH
MUNCH

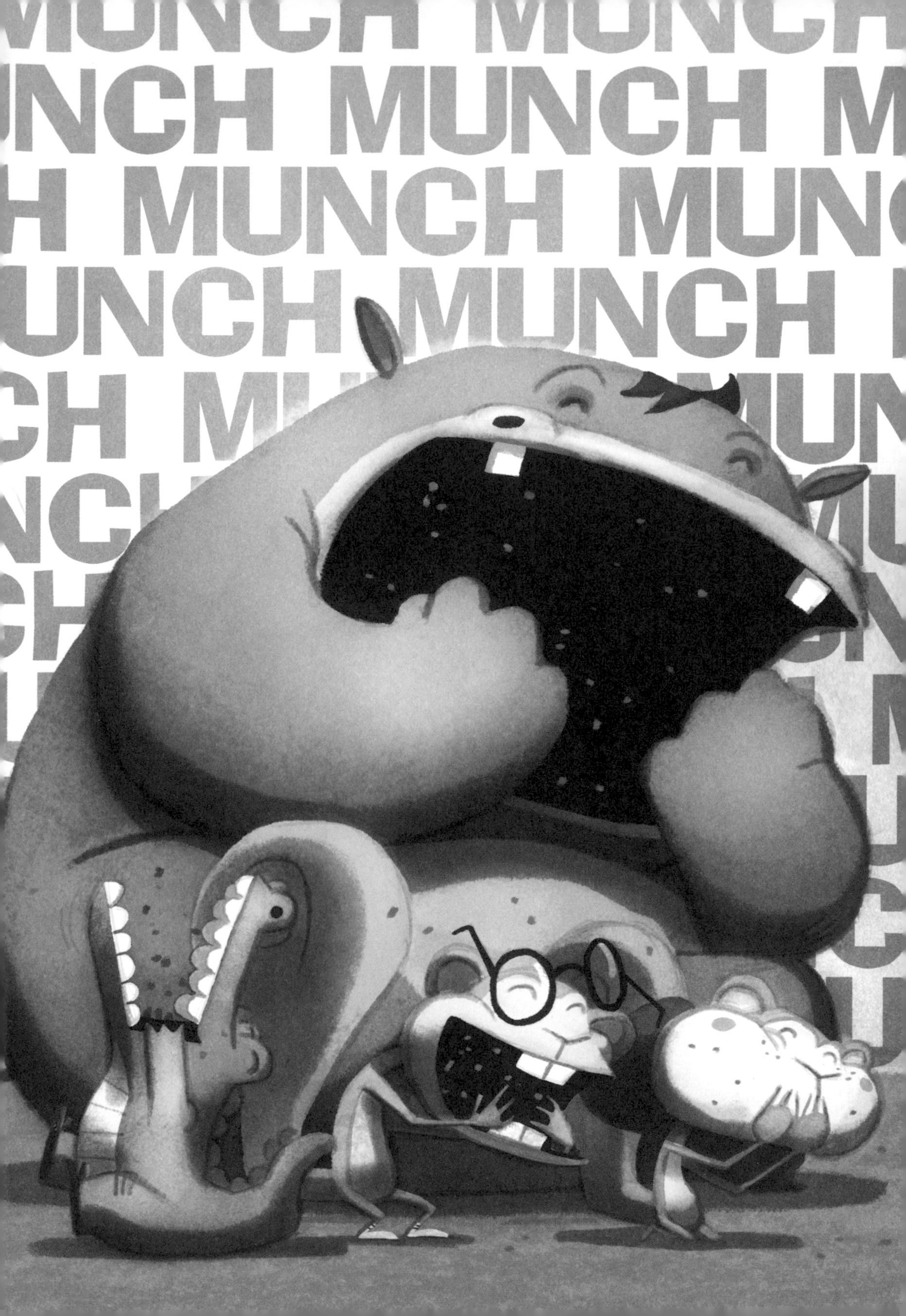
MUNCH MUNCH
MUNCH
MUNCH
MUNCH

First Edition, September 2016   •   5 7 9 10 8 6 4   •   FAC-034274-18017 • Printed in the United States of America
Reinforced binding
This book is set in Century 725/Monotype; Ad Lib/Fontspring; Grilled Cheese BTN/Fontbros

Library of Congress Cataloging-in-Publication Data
Names: Willems, Mo, author, illustrator. | Santat, Dan, author, illustrator.
Title: The cookie fiasco / by [Mo Willems and] Dan Santat.
Description: First edition. | Los Angeles ; New York : Hyperion Books for Children, an imprint of Disney Book Group, [2016] | Series: Elephant & Piggie like reading! | Summary: "There are only three cookies and four hungry friends to share them with. This is not good. This is not equal! How are they ever going to solve this fiasco?!"—Provided by publisher.
Identifiers: LCCN 2015042551 | ISBN 9781484726365 (hardback)
Subjects: | CYAC: Sharing—Fiction. | Division—Fiction. | Cookies—Fiction. | Friendship—Fiction. | Animals—Fiction. | Humorous stories. | BISAC: JUVENILE FICTION / Humorous Stories. | JUVENILE FICTION / Concepts / General. | JUVENILE FICTION / Social Issues / Values & Virtues.
Classification: LCC PZ7.W65535 Co 2016 | DDC [E]—dc23
LC record available at http://lccn.loc.gov/2015042551

Visit hyperionbooksforchildren.com and pigeonpresents.com

Now I
am thirsty
for milk!

**Elephant & Piggie
also like reading:**

We Are Growing!
by Laurie Keller
(Theodor Seuss Geisel Medal)

The Good for Nothing Button!
by Charise Mericle Harper

It's Shoe Time!
by Bryan Collier